WINNI ALLFOURS

WINNI ALLFOURS

Babette Cole

PUFFIN BOOKS

Winni Allfours wanted a pony more than anything
else in the world.

There were ponies by the bus-stop.

Winni always missed
the school bus.

"Please," pleaded Winni.
"No!" said her mum and dad
(who had a very strict life-style
and only ate vegetables).
"We don't approve
of people who
own ponies."

"But I only want
a little one!"
said Winni.

"I don't want to hear any more about it," said her mum. "Sit down and eat your vegetables."

"And no more of those nasty hamburgers and chips for school dinner!" said her dad.

"You'll turn into a horse if you carry on eating that many carrots," said the school dinner lady.

"What a brilliant idea!" said Winni.

So Winni ate and ate.
She ate up all her vegetables.
"Good girl!" said her mum and dad.

Very slowly

to

things started

happen...

Her parents were horrified.
"She's eating my lawn and flower beds!"
said her dad.

"What are we going to do?" shrieked her mum.
"She's ruined the organic vegetable patch!"
"Serves them right!"
said Winni.

But Winni knew just what to do.

She jumped the wall and joined the bus-stop ponies!

She loved racing around with them.

"Hey, Winni," said her new friend, Snowdrop, "you're real fast. You should meet my owner, Paddy. He's a racehorse trainer!"

"Good heavens," said Paddy, when he saw
Winni run. "She's a Grand National winner!"

So he took Winni off to Newmarket to start training to be a racehorse.

"This is much better than school!" said Winni.

"You should be very proud
of your daughter," said Paddy.
But her parents were still horrified.

Mr and Mrs Allfours were not, however, the only people watching Winni run.

Nobbler O'Toole, the horse dealer, wanted to buy Winni so that he could sell her for lots of money. "Certainly not!" said her mum. "We couldn't possibly sell our daughter!"

So the night before the Grand National,
Nobbler sent his lads to steal Winni.

But when they stopped at the pub, Winni stole the lorry! "That's no ordinary horse!" they said.

She drove straight to the race-track.
Luckily, her parents had come to watch.
"Come on, Dad!" said Winni. "I need your help!"

"Hang on, Dad!" said Winni, as they flew past the winning post.

Dad was scared stiff!
But they beat the world record.

Winni won pots of money for everyone.
But her dad had a
very sore bottom!

"If we gave you lots of hamburgers and chips to eat," said her mum, "you would change back into a little girl and we'd promise to buy you a pony."

"And go back to school!" said Winni.
"No thanks, this is
far more fun!"